Peter Pan

Edited by Stella Croker

Longmeadow Press

The Darling family lived in London, in a nice big house with a backyard. There were six of them: Mr Darling, Mrs Darling and their children. Wendy was the first, then came John, then Michael. There was also Nana, the children's nurse, Nana was a dog. She proved to be quite a treasure of a nurse. She served the children's breakfast, helped them finish all the food on their plates and gave them candies. She also had them learn their school-lessons and she looked after them when their parents were out for the evening. One night Mr and Mrs Darling were planning to go to the theater.

Mr Darling was getting dressed and everything had gone well until he had come to his tie. Although quite a clever man, Mr Darling had never entirely mastered the art of putting his tie on. This was always an extremely unpleasant matter to him and only Mrs Darling was able to calm him when this happened. "This tie will never tie! Who has been playing with it?" Mr Darling shouted. "How many times do I have to say that I don't want anyone to play with my ties!"

"No one played with your tie, father," Wendy ventured to say, but that only infuriated her father more.

"I'm your father and when I say something I'm right. Is that clear? Parents are always right," he continued. "Besides children are not supposed to argue. Children here, children there! That's all I hear! I want you to grow up in a hurry and, first of all, no more nurse!" And with these words, poor Nana was sent outside to her kennel. To forget how unhappy they were without her, John and Michael started playing together.

"I'm Peter Pan and you're Captain Hook. Let's fight!" John said.

"You thought you would escape, Peter, but you're caught!" answered Michael, as they jumped around with their cardboard swords.

Mr Darling was much too practical to believe in
fairies, gnomes or even in Peter Pan. "Nonsense! You'd
better be good, listen to what you're told and work hard
in school!" he said. Mrs Darling, as a child, had believed
in Peter Pan, but that was a long time ago and she
hardly remembered him now. But as far as Wendy was
concerned, Peter Pan was very definitely real. Look,
here he is crossing the bedroom in one leap! Wendy
isn't very surprised to see him back because the last
time Peter Pan came to tell her of his latest adventures,
Nana stole his shadow. Now he's come back to find it,
but the shadow is running away.

"Ouch! Who's pulling my hair?" squealed Wendy.

It was Tinker Bell, the little fairy who followed Peter Pan wherever he went. Peter Pan finally caught his shadow and Wendy offered to sew it back on. "You know what father told us, he wants us to be grown ups, but we won't. It's much more fun to be children and be able to play," Wendy told Peter Pan.

"Don't worry," said Peter, "if you follow me, you won't have to be grown ups. I know a country where children never grow up. It's a lot of fun," said Peter giving her a kiss.

"I'll take you there," he offered, "and your brothers can come along too."

"But how can we get there?" Wendy asked.

"That's very simple, all you've got to do is fly," Peter told her. Wendy looked astonished.

"We can't fly, we don't know how to," she said with disappointment.

"Oh yes, you can, just try!" Peter suggested, and Wendy discovered to her own amazement that she really could fly. Of course at the beginning she wasn't quite as graceful as Peter, but she soon was able to follow him. "Let's wake your brothers up! We must leave before twelve o'clock," urged Peter. A few minutes later four little shadows could be seen flying way up in the sky.

They flew all night long to
the Neverland where there
were magic shores, big
forests and pirates. There
was a big boat anchored in
the bay. This was Captain
Hook's ship.

14

The Captain had two
enemies, one was Peter Pan
and the other was the
crocodile. One day, while
fighting with Peter, the
Captain had his hand cut off
and the crocodile greedily
swallowed it. He would have
liked very much to have
more since he liked the taste
of the hand. So he always
followed the captain around
in case he could get another
bite!

Captain Hook had a very sharp eye and as soon as he saw Peter Pan flying over the ship, he shouted: "Prepare for action. Get your guns ready to shoot. I'll get that boy this time!" Peter, Wendy and the boys were resting on a big cloud when 'Boom!' there was a big explosion and the cloud was split in two by a bullet shot from the ship. "Tinker, go ahead, show them the way," said Peter Pan. "I must have a few words with my old friend, Captain Hook."

Tinker Bell had agreed, but she really only did what pleased her. She guided Wendy and her brothers for a while, but then she suddenly disappeared and there was no more light, no more fairy. She'd vanished. "Tinker Bell, where are you? Wait for us! Wait!" The children screamed for help, but no-one answered their calls.

Tinker Bell had made up her mind that she hated Wendy because Wendy was taking Peter Pan's attention away from her: "I hate you! I hate you and as far as I'm concerned, you can be lost," Tinker Bell snapped. She dived down into a clump of trees on the island. Every part of the island was so familiar to her that she could have found her way with her eyes closed.

She very soon spotted a big tree and she let herself down through a hardly-visible opening in the trunk to where the Lost Boys lived. Peter was their leader and they were waiting for him to come back from his expedition to earth. "Hi Tinker! What are you up to? Where's Peter?" one of the boys asked. Tinker explained that he would be back soon.

She also said, "A big bird in a night-gown is trying to get in here, and I think we'd better kill that foolish bird, because we don't want anybody in here, right?" And all the boys gathered together outside.

When they saw Wendy and her brothers flying by, they took their catapults out and started shooting stones at them. Wendy got hit by a big stone and she was falling rapidly when Peter appeared just in time to catch her. "Peter, you saved my life!" she exclaimed, throwing her arms around Peter's neck. Tinker Bell was so jealous that she thought she would scream, but she was careful not to be seen by Peter.

"Is that the way you welcome my friends!" said Peter. "I was bringing you a mother to tell you stories!" He was very angry with the boys.

"How could we have known; Tinker was the one who warned us about a strange bird!" the boys answered, rather ashamed of themselves.

"Tinker, where are you, you little rascal? Ah, here you are! Is that true, did you really lie to the boys?" Peter Pan demanded. Tinker Bell didn't answer, but her face gave her away. "Be gone! I don't want you here any more! Do you understand? Go away!" said Peter in a fury.

When Tinker Bell was gone, all the boys asked Peter to forgive her. Even Wendy didn't resent the little fairy for what she had done. "All right, all right! I'll go and look for her in a few days," Peter agreed. Then to help Wendy forget what had happened, Peter and the boys took her to the Mermaids' lagoon.

The children often spent long summer days in this
lagoon, swimming or floating and playing
mermaids' games in the water most of the time. The
jungle was so full of wonderful animals and other things.

There were also strange
noises, but what the children
didn't know was that some
wild Indians were
surrounding them.

"Look, there's a big
footprint in the sand!" John
said.

"It is very big, indeed!"
added one of the Lost Boys.

Just then an arrow
whistled from behind them
and was imbedded in a tree.

Soon enough they were to
find out that there was a
fierce tribe of Indians in the
jungle. They carried
tomahawks and knives and
their bodies gleamed with
paint and oil.

At first crouching behind
the trees, the Indians all
jumped out together on the
children and made them
prisoners.

The children were carried away and tied to a big totem pole. The Indians began playing the tom-tom and singing war songs. Little Michael began crying and although the others managed not to cry, they also felt very frightened. "That's only to scare us. They don't mean to do anything to us," John said, trying to convince himself.

"Who says we don't mean it?" the big chief jeered. "Where is Tiger Lily? If she isn't back by tonight, you'll be burnt!" Things certainly didn't seem too good, even John felt his teeth chattering.

Meanwhile Peter Pan and Wendy, who had gone off on their own, had reached the mermaids' lagoon. "Oh Peter, it's so pretty here. The water is crystal clear," exclaimed Wendy."It's almost like dreaming!"

"It's real though," Peter assured her. "Come up on the cliff and look over here!" Peter helped Wendy to climb up and when she stood on the top of the cliff she was able to see all the mermaids resting, playing or combing their hair.

The mermaids loved to bask in the sun or to dive into the water with a big splash. Peter often came to have a chat with them and they liked him. "Won't you join us, Peter?" they asked when they saw him. Suddenly there was a strange noise.

"Pirates!" Peter cried and they rushed to hide behind the cliff.

"It's Hook. He's captured the Indian chief's daughter, Tiger Lily. Poor Lily! We've got to help her," Peter decided.

"Where are they going?" Wendy asked.

"They're taking her to that big rock, the one in the shape of a skull," Peter explained.

Peter and Wendy saw the pirate dinghy pass close
by. There were three figures visible, Hook, one of the
pirates, named Smee and Tiger Lily. Her wrists and
ankles were tied. It seemed that they had brought her to
the rock to die when the tide rose. Peter and Wendy
listened carefully to what the pirates said.

Captain Hook began by warning Tiger Lily: "If you won't be reasonable and tell us where Peter and the boys hide, we will have no choice but to leave you here and you know what will happen then. The water will slowly come up first to your knees, then to your arms and your chest and, finally, to your head. Then there will be nothing for you to do," Captain Hook grinned, "but to drown!"

"I will not give you any information," Tiger Lily answered with a very determined expression.

"Watch this, Wendy!" Peter jumped up in the air and landed on Captain Hook's boat. When Hook saw him, he was overcome with rage and pulled his sword out, but Peter was so fast that he jumped on the blade and bounced up and down as if he was on a spring.

The fight that followed was fierce and neither Peter nor Hook would relent. "Prepare to meet your doom, proud youth!" snarled the terrifying Captain Hook.

Peter, with a strange smile on his face, answered "Dark and cruel man, this will be the end of all your evil deeds!" Spurred on by these words, Hook started fighting with even more determination. Just when he was about to win, he heard a ticking sound, which he knew was the crocodile who had swallowed a clock. He was so scared that he lost his balance and had it not been for his hook, he would have fallen right into the crocodile's wide open jaws.

"I'm coming Captain, I'm coming! Hold on!" Smee was rowing as hard as he could, for the Captain's hook was only saving him from falling down for a few minutes. Hook was in a most precarious situation and not until then had he realized how strong and muscular a crocodile's jaw is.

46

While Hook was fighting for his life, Peter swam to Tiger Lily and saved her just in time. All he could see was a little feather pointing out of the water! "You must have been scared to death!" Peter said.

"I'm so thankful you were here," answered Lily.

Captain Hook had barely escaped the crocodile's jaws one more time and Smee was rowing as quickly as possible back to the ship. Peter flew away, carrying Tiger Lily in his arms and Wendy followed them to the Indian village.

When they got to the
village the first thing they
did was to go to say 'hello'
to Big Chief, Lily's father.
Peter waved his hand in
greeting and Lily threw
herself into her father's arms.
Then Peter and the Chief sat
together in the tepee and
Peter wore a big feather-
headdress.

The children were set free and joined in the festivities. The Indians started playing the tom-tom and a dance was held around the totem pole.

Everybody was very happy, except Wendy who sat to one side thinking that Peter hadn't paid any attention to her since he had saved Tiger Lily's life.

"Boys, time to go!" Peter said after the celebration had gone on for a while. All the children headed back home, singing joyfully:

"Peter Pan is the strongest and the quickest.

Peter Pan is as fast as an arrow, as light as a flake of snow.

We'd follow him anywhere, for more adventures."

Tinker Bell, still in exile, had plenty of time to brood on her misfortunes. She would quite happily have settled for revenge. The only problem was that she couldn't think of anything. As for Captain Hook, he also would have liked to settle the score with Peter Pan and as soon as he caught sight of Tinker, he had an idea. "Smee, catch her," commanded the scheming Hook, "she may help us do what we want!" Smee took off his cap and managed to trap the little fairy in it.

"Captain Hook would be delighted to have a chat with you, Miss Tinker!" he chuckled.

The Captain had put on
his Sunday best hook and
clothes. "Welcome aboard,
Miss Tinker!" he sneered.
"It's a pleasure to be able to
entertain such a charming
lady. It came to our ears that
you and Peter Pan weren't
on such good terms
anymore. That's too bad,
Peter is such a nice boy,
somewhat bad-tempered we
don't deny," he went on,
"but he certainly doesn't
mean any harm. I would be
inclined to say that since
that girl Wendy arrived
things have gone from bad
to worse. She is the one who
is responsible.

All I want is to get rid of that girl. So if you would tell me where she and Peter are hiding, we might easily send her back to where she comes from. Don't you agree?" The captain was very convincing and Tinker didn't hesitate to point out the boys' hiding place in the forest when he showed her a map of the island. "Thank you very much, little brat," gloated Hook. "That's all I wanted to know! Between you and me, that Peter Pan of yours isn't worth a penny now that I know where he hides! He is very fortunate having friends like you!" And the captain burst into laughter. Tinker was locked up in a glass cage as a reward.

Meanwhile Wendy and the boys were back home in the forest and Wendy was telling stories. They were all listening carefully and you could have heard a fly buzz!

The stories that she was telling were very sad and the boys found it almost impossible not to cry. Just outside the tree, the pirates were getting ready to attack when they started listening to Wendy. They, too, found it difficult not to cry when Wendy began to speak of her mother and of all mothers.

When she was finished, all the boys clamoured, "We want to go back to our mothers!"

"You can go, if you want, I'm not holding you here," Peter Pan replied, "But I warn you, if you go back to earth, you'll grow up and you'll never be able to come back to Neverland!" The Lost Boys didn't wait any longer. It seemed to them that even growing up wouldn't be all that bad if you had a mother to care about you. So they all flew away.

Wendy stayed a little longer saying, "I promise never to forget you, Peter Pan, but, you see, children need their mothers. You should come with us too."

Peter didn't answer so Wendy left, but to her great dismay as soon as she was outside she discovered that all the boys had been captured by the pirates. When Captain Hook saw Wendy he shouted: "Grab her and tie her up!" So poor Wendy suffered the same fate as the others.

She was tied up with big ropes and the pirates each took one of the children on their backs and started walking through the dark forest.

The pirates carried their
prisoners onto the ship.
"Whoever makes the first
move will be in trouble!"
growled one of the pirates.
They proceeded to tie the
children to the big mast.
"Oh no! Not again!" the
boys thought and even
though things had turned out
well with the Indians, they
were very scared when they
heard the pirates singing:
"Avast belay, yo ho,
heave to,
A-pirating we go;
And if we're parted by a shot
We're sure to meet below!
Avast, belay, when I appear,
By fear they're overtook;
Naught's left upon your bones
When you have shaken
claws with Hook."

Hook was presiding at one
end of the ship and all the
pirates sang in chorus, lifting
their flag high in the air.

They were a very
frightening bunch to look at,
with their deeply-furrowed
faces, their rough features
and their fierce expressions.
The children huddled up
against each other.

"Untie them and bring them to me!" Captain Hook ordered. The children couldn't believe what they had heard.

Smee then announced that they would be saved on one condition: "The captain appreciates your good points, he thinks you're cunning and clever and therefore offers you the chance to become pirates."

In the meantime, Tinker
Bell had enough time to
think over her bad behaviour
and how she had been
punished. She had heard all
that Hook said and
understood that she had
been cheated. She made up
her mind that she must
make up for being so
naughty, so she crashed into
the glass door of her prison
and broke it.

Back in the forest, Peter continued playing his flute for a while after all the children had left. Then he got up and happened to bump into a big package that had been left there intentionally by the pirates. There was a little note on the present which read: "To Peter Pan, with love from Wendy."

Peter was very curious to see what it was, but when he put it to his ear, he heard something clicking inside.

Tinker, who had flown as quickly as she could, was just in time to grab the package from his hands gasping:

"Throw it away! Peter, throw it away!"

She had hardly finished the sentence, when the package, which had a bomb inside, exploded. Fortunately neither of them got hurt. When Peter stood up after the commotion was over, he immediately looked for Tinker, hoping that she was all right too.

"Peter you must hurry. Wendy and the children have been made prisoners by the pirates and they will be put to death unless you can save them!" she said as soon as she recovered. Peter was very proud of her, but he knew he had no time to waste.

On the pirates' ship things had become very serious. "Now it's time to decide what you would like best," grinned the detestable Hook, "Staying with me and the boat, or going to the bottom of the ocean. What's your choice, gentlemen?" he asked.

The boys might have been tempted to become pirates, but Wendy had decided otherwise. "What, Lost Boys, you would betray Peter Pan! Shame on you!" she said and, lowering her voice, she added: "I'm sure Peter will save us, one way or another. Captain, we're ready when you are. We prefer to die!" she said, bravely walking out to the plank from which they were to jump to the dark waters below.

Everybody was holding his breath. Then Wendy jumped and she fell, but, to all the pirates' surprise, there was no sound of her hitting the water and no splash. "No splash!" Smee exclaimed.

"What did you say? No splash!" Hook repeated. Peter had been hiding by the side of the boat, holding on to some ropes and when Wendy had jumped he had caught her in midair.

"I was so sure you would come!" Wendy said.

Peter helped Wendy to a safe place and then he leapt up onto the deck. Thus Hook found himself once again face-to-face with Peter. The others drew back, forming a circle around the two enemies. "Peter! Peter!" The Lost Boys hailed him.

"I'll kill you myself with this sword, since even bombs cannot kill you!" Hook cried.

Without any more words they began fighting. Both of them were brilliant swordsmen and parried rapidly. Hook lunged forward his sword aiming at Peter, but Peter was quicker and the blade, instead of piercing him, stuck into the mast.

"Get me another sword at once!" Captain Hook
screamed. As soon as he was handed one, he hurled
himself on Peter, who once again escaped the blow.
Peter darted and lunged without showing any sign of
being tired.

Finally Peter, with a clever thrust, threw Captain
Hook's hat high into the air.

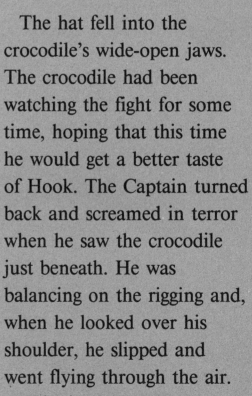

The hat fell into the crocodile's wide-open jaws. The crocodile had been watching the fight for some time, hoping that this time he would get a better taste of Hook. The Captain turned back and screamed in terror when he saw the crocodile just beneath. He was balancing on the rigging and, when he looked over his shoulder, he slipped and went flying through the air.

This time there was a splash!

Now Peter was the only one who could be captain of the boat, since the ex-captain was now swimming as fast as he could, behind a dinghy rowed by a few members of his crew who didn't want Peter Pan as their captain. The crocodile followed closely behind.

On the boat everyone was excited: "Go ahead Tinker! Turn this dreary boat into a fairyland ship!" Peter called out and Tinker Bell, flying above the deck, the hull and the sails, sprinkled gold powder over everything.

What happened next was most unusual, even in Neverland. The boat, which had become a beautiful glowing golden color and as light as a feather, was carried by the wind up into the sky. There it was quite clearly to be seen sailing proudly through the sky.

It floated high above the bay, above the forest. The Indians couldn't believe their eyes when the ship went by. It drifted for what seemed a long time. "Did you hear it?" Michael suddenly screamed.

"Hear what?" his sister asked.

"Big Ben!" he replied enthusiastically.

"We're back home."

When the Darlings got home, they found the three children asleep in the most peculiar places. Wendy was on the window sill, Michael was at the foot of his bed and John was holding his Sunday hat on his chest.

When Mr and Mrs Darling woke the children up to put them back in their beds, Wendy, Michael and John all chattered excitedly of their wonderful adventures in the Neverland.

"Peter Pan took us there and we met the Lost Boys.
We invited them over here, but they preferred to stay on
the boat with Peter. Then we were made prisoner by the
Indians and after that by the pirates, but Peter saved us
both times," Wendy explained.

Of course Mr Darling didn't believe all this and he
said: "I guess I'll have to wait a while before you're
grown ups. It seems, after all, we do need Nana," and
he went to bring her back into the nursery.

They all looked out of the window and they quite
distinctly could see the shadow of a big ship cast over
the moon. "That's Peter's ship! They're going back to
the Neverland!" John exclaimed.

This edition produced exclusively for
Longmeadow Press
by Twin Books

ISBN 0-681-40104-4

Printed in Hong Kong